My Very First Look at

My Home

CHANHASSEN, MINNESOTA • LONDON

www.two-canpublishing.com

Published in the United States and Canada by
Two-Can Publishing
18705 Lake Drive East, Chanhassen, MN 55317

Conceived, designed and edited by

Picthall & Gunzi Ltd

21A Widmore Road, Bromley, Kent BR1 1RW

Original concept: Chez Picthall
Editor: Margaret Hynes
Designer: Paul Calver
Photography: Steve Gorton
Additional photographs: Daniel Pangbourne
DTP: Tony Cutting, Ray Bryant

Two-Can Publishing is a division of Creative Publishing international, Inc.
18705 Lake Drive East, Chanhassen, MN 55317
1-800-328-3895
www.two-canpublishing.com

ISBN 1-58728-671-8 (HC)
ISBN 1-58728-685-8 (SC)
ISBN 1-58728-579-7 (ALB)

2 4 6 8 10 9 7 5 3 1

Color reproduction by Reed Digital.
Printed in Hong Kong

key: b = bottom, c = centre, l = left, r = right, t = top):

The publisher would like to thank the following people, companies and organizations for their kind permission to reproduce their photographs:

Multiyork: 10br, 11bl; **Robert Bosch Limited**: 4tl, 21br; **Sony UK**: 10br, 11tl, 24tl

My Very First Look at
My Home

Christiane Gunzi

TWO CAN™

CHANHASSEN, MINNESOTA • LONDON

In the kitchen

oven

saucepan

spoon

kettle

glass

Can you find the yellow spoon?

teapot

fork

plate

apron

knife

cup

oven mitts

Point to the cup with flowers!

Food and drink

strawberries

apple

orange juice

pizza

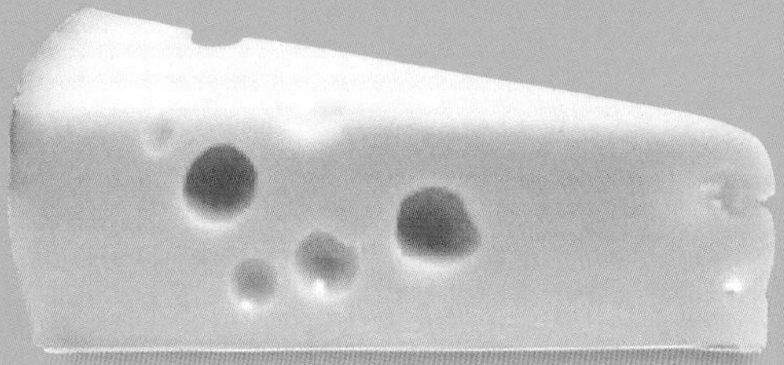

cheese

Can you count the strawberries?

pasta

bananas

bagel

milk

hamburger

How many drinks are there?

Birthday baking

birthday candles

sugar

wooden spoon

cookie cutters

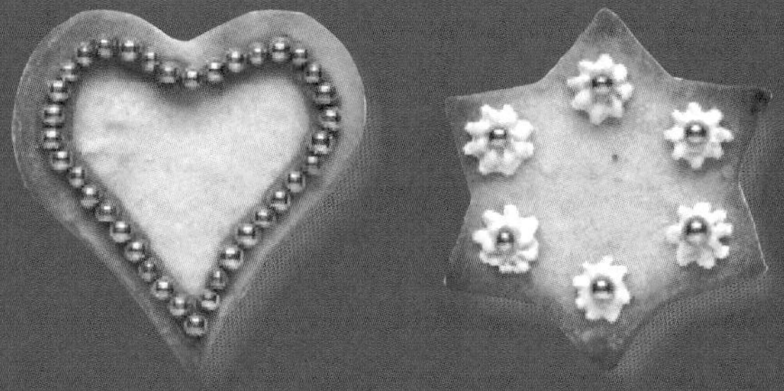

cookies

Count the birthday candles!

butter

eggs

mixing bowl

flour

birthday cake

What shape are the eggs?

In the living room

book

clock

picture

coffee table

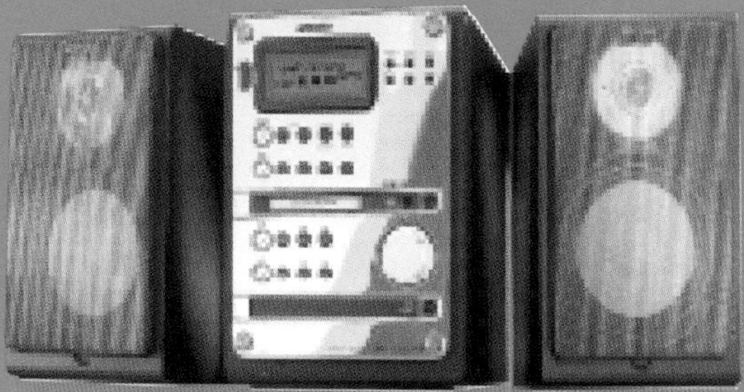

stereo system

What animal is in the picture?

television

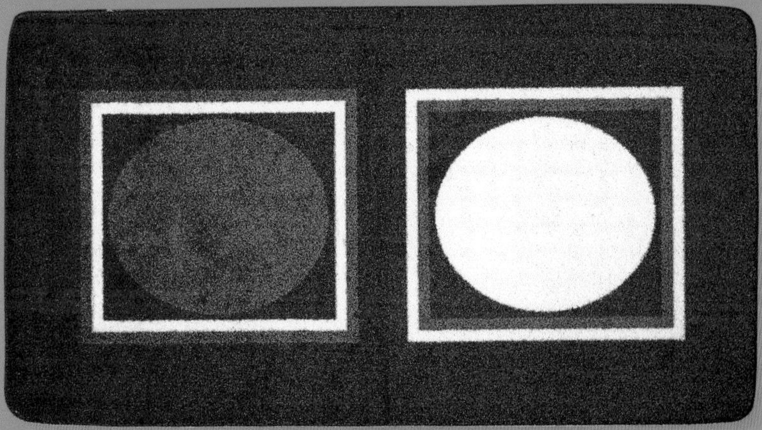

rug

sofa

flowers

Can you sit on any of these things?

In the playroom

whiteboard

robot

checkers

crayons

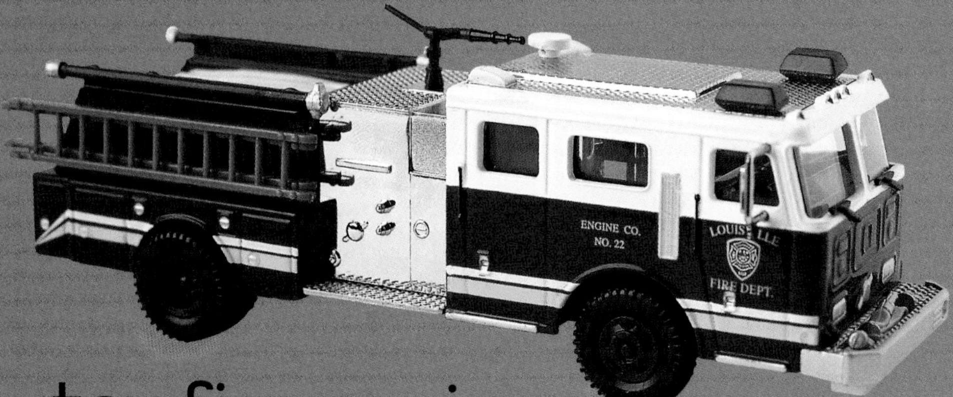

toy fire engine

What does a firefighter drive?

modeling clay

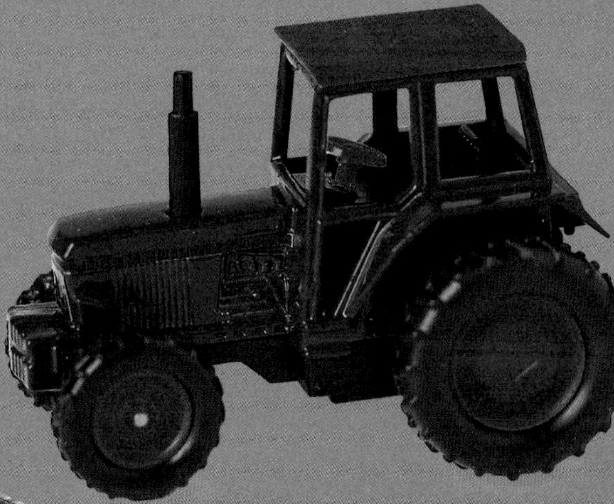

toy tractor

toy chest

doll

toy drum

Can you find the robot?

In the bedroom

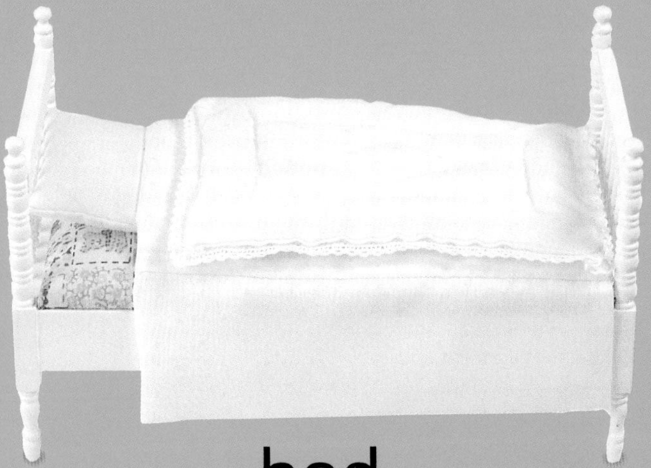

bed

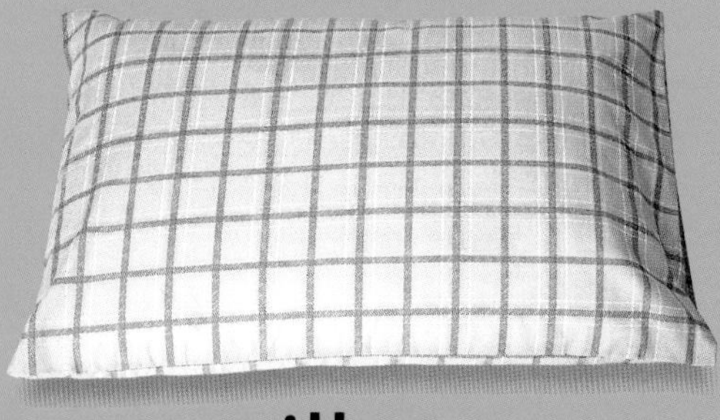

pillow

blanket

pajamas

What do you wear in bed?

wardrobe

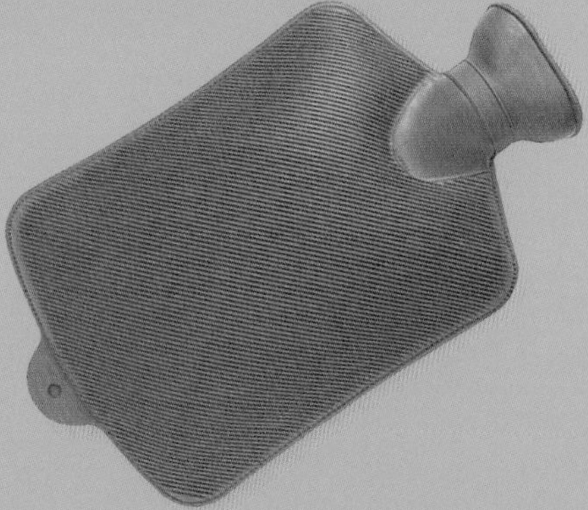
hot-water bottle

teddy bear

slippers

lamp

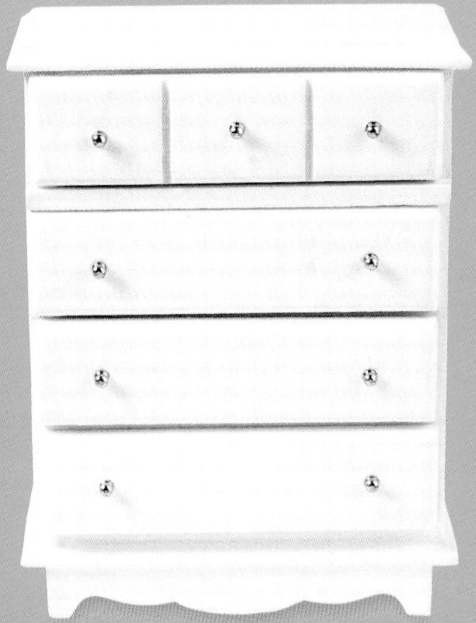
chest of drawers

Where is the teddy bear?

In the bathroom

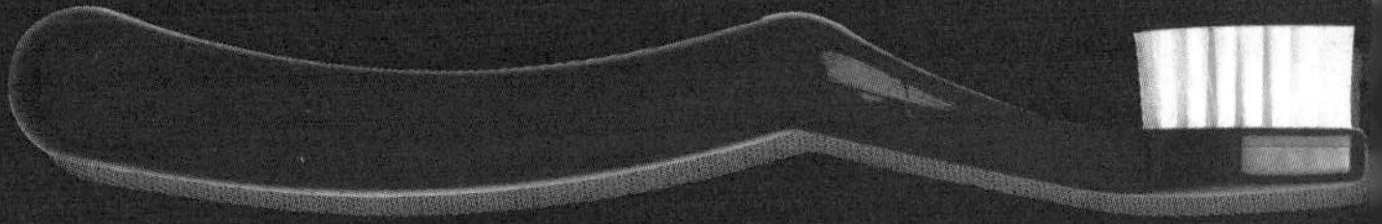

toothbrush

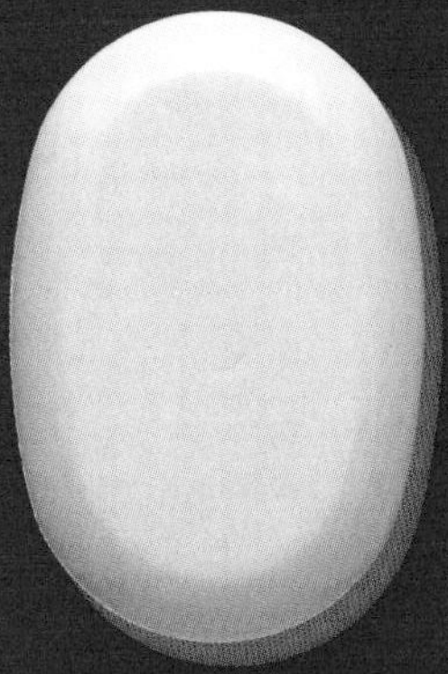

soap

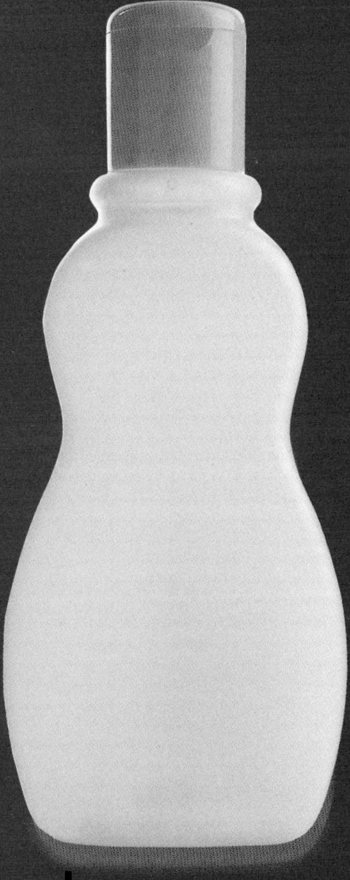

shampoo

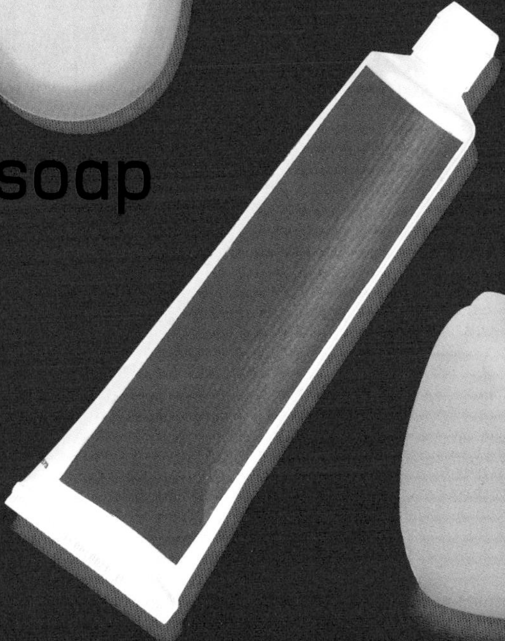

toothpaste

toy duck

How many bath toys are there?

Point to the striped towel!

Around the home

coins

keys

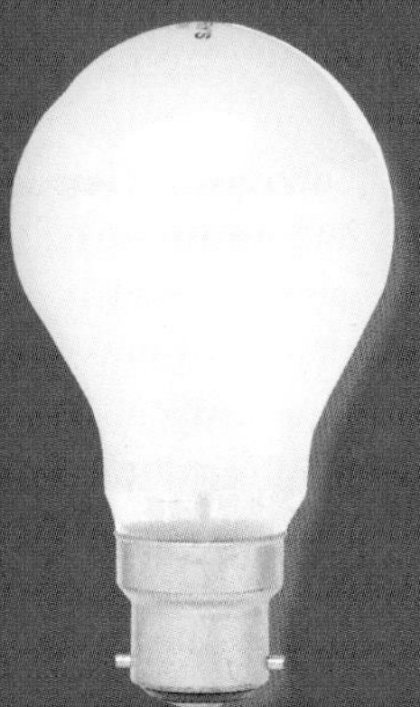

bulb

candle

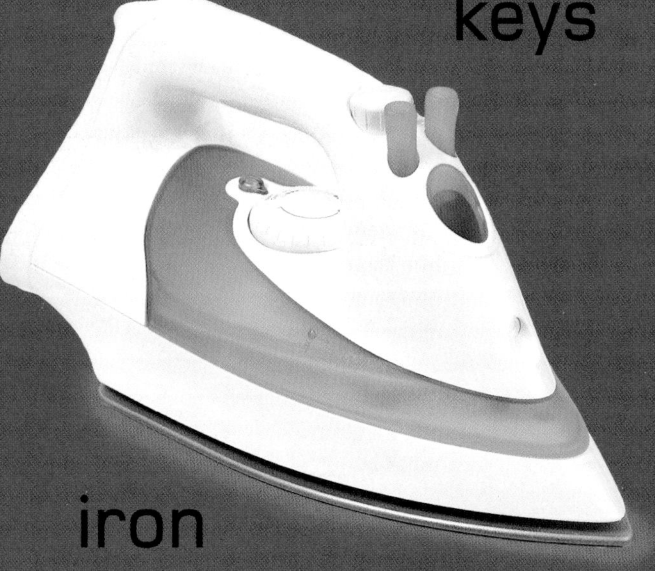

iron

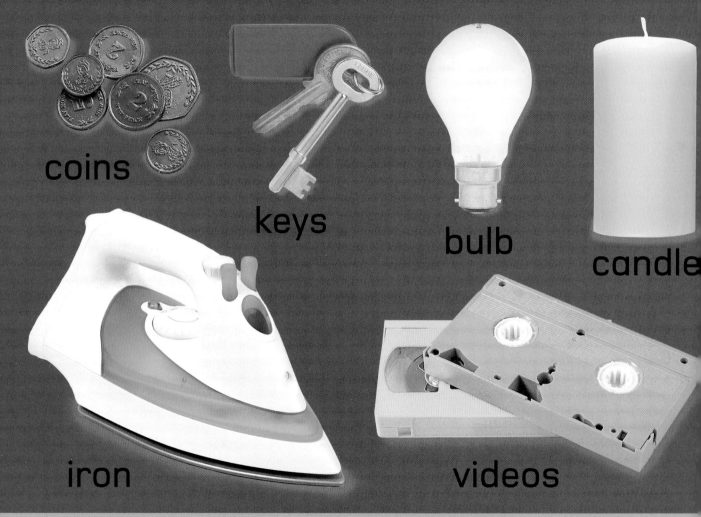

videos

How many coins are there?

scissors

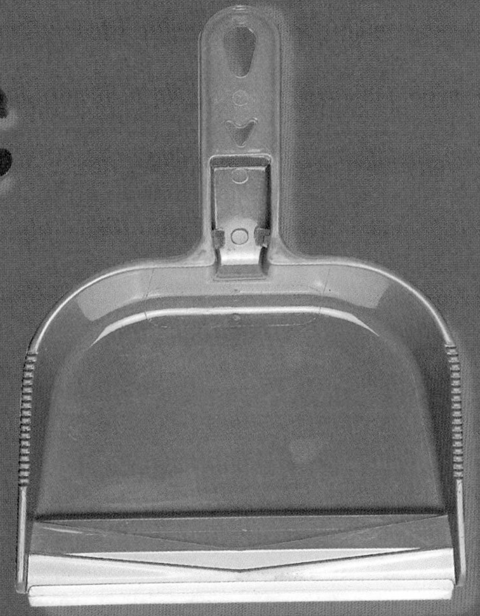

dustpan

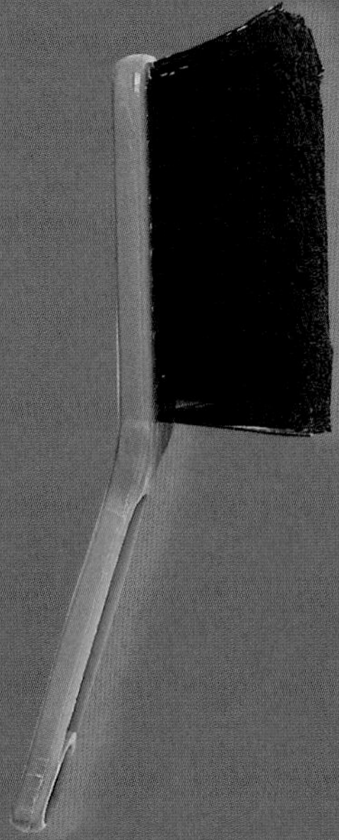

brush

telephone

compact disc

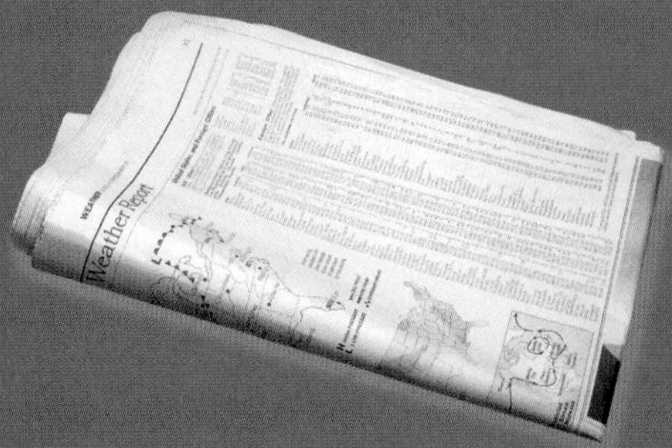

newspaper

What color is the dustpan?

In the garden

rose

leaf

sticks

pebbles

pine cone

flowerpots

Can you count the pebbles?

butterfly

sunflower

ant

fork

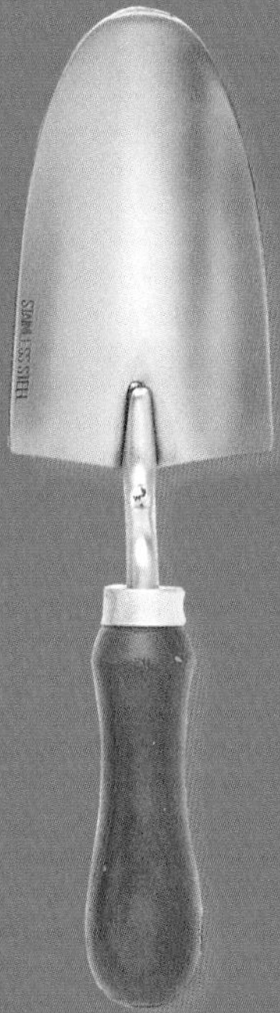

trowel

lawn mower

Point to the orange flower!

In the toolshed

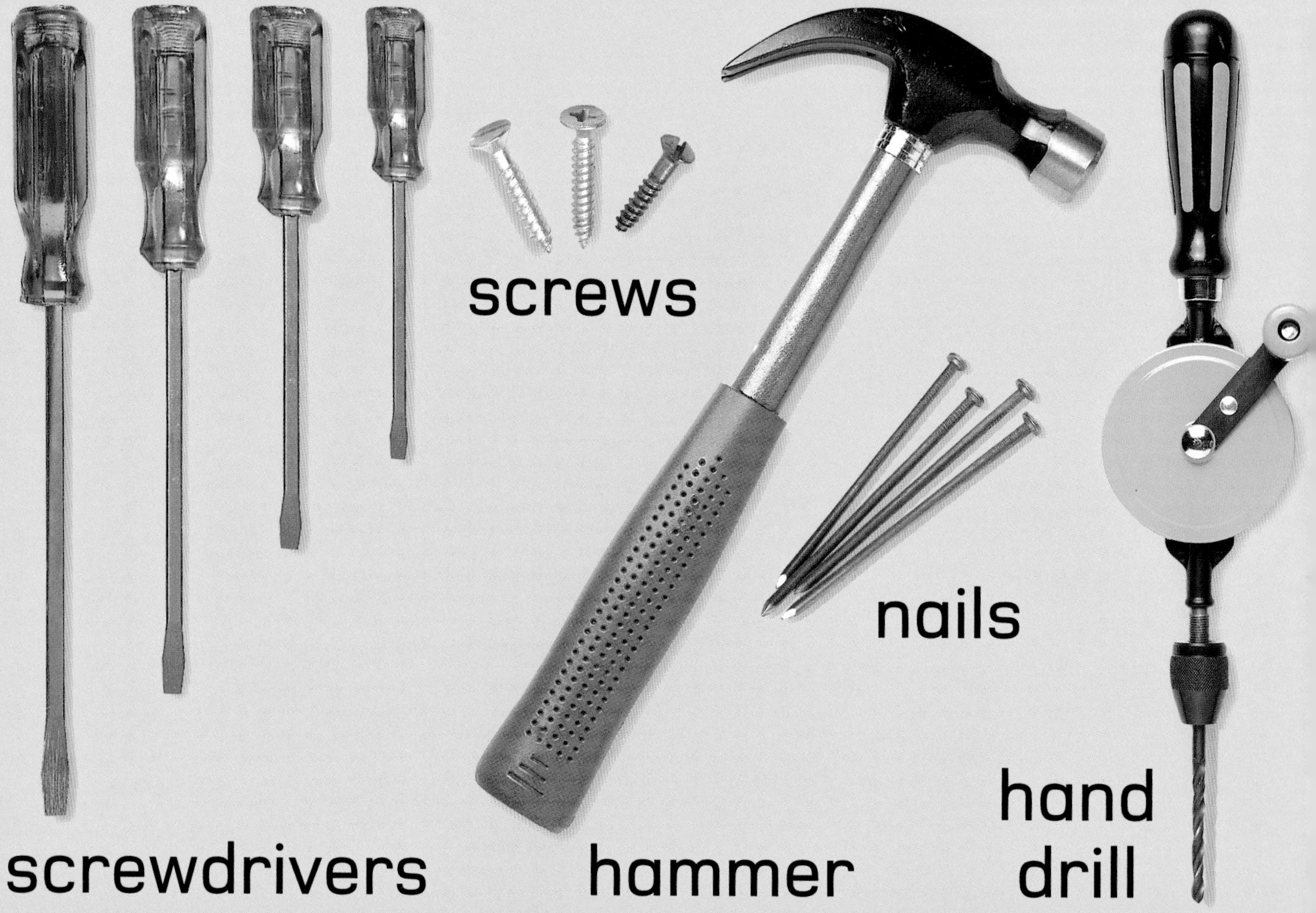

How many screws can you see?

sticky tape

tape measure

paintbrushes

paint can

saw

What shape is the sticky tape?

In which room?

television

oven mitts

toy drum

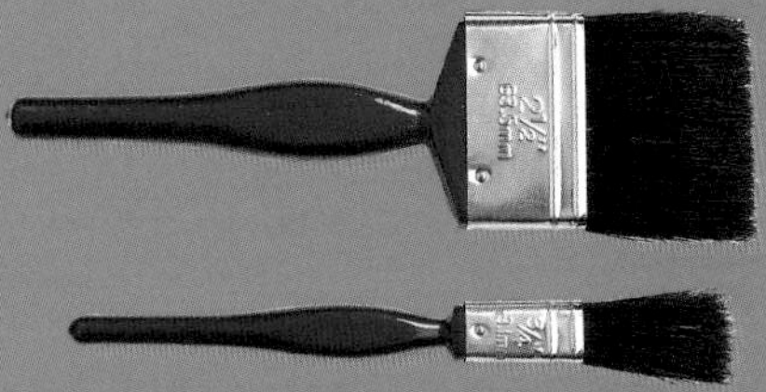

paintbrushes

toy duck

blanket

Where do you use oven mitts?